My Stories by Hildy Calpurnia Rose

By Dale Gottlieb

Alfred A. Knopf New York

THIS IS A BORZOI BOOK
PUBLISHED BY ALFRED A. KNOPF, INC.

Library of Congress Cataloging-in-Publication Data
Gottlieb, Dale.
My Stories by Hildy Calpurnia Rose / by Dale Gottlieb.
p.   cm. Summary: A young girl keeps a journal about the people
and events in her life.
ISBN 0-679-81150-8 (trade) — ISBN 0-679-91150-2 (lib. bdg.)
[1. Brooklyn (New York, N.Y.) — Fiction. 2. Diaries — Fiction.]
I. Title. PZ7. G696St   1991   [Fic] — dc20   90-46096   CIP   AC

Manufactured in Singapore
2 4 6 8 0 9 7 5 3 1
Book Design by Edward Miller

For Robopop Chris,
Blake, and Hill,
and for my family and friends
who gave me these stories

Thanks to my editor/mentor,
Anne Schwartz
And thanks, Bandini

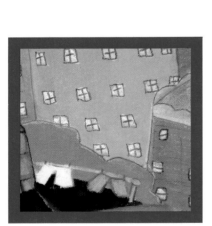

Contents

Dear Reader,

Eight years ago I was born on a hot Sunday night on the last day of August right here in Brooklyn, New York. My name is Hildy Calpurnia Rose. Hildy, after my mother's favorite uncle, Hilden, and Calpurnia, from my father's favorite book, *Hickory Tree Summer.* Dad's always reading. He says that it's a way to see how other people really think and feel; that when you read about a character, it's like stepping into their shoes.

I put myself in someone's shoes by writing about them. All kinds of thoughts fly through my head—it's like looking deep inside them and me at the same time—and I swear I can hear their voices. Sometimes I don't like the person any better. But sometimes I do.

I have a new journal to write about my people in. My parents' friends Arnold and Marisa sent it to me from Italy. It's this beautiful book with marbleized paper on the cover and leather corners. I love the way it smells, too, like a really old library book. I've almost filled the pages with seven new stories and drawings!

So here's my journal. I hope when you read it, you'll get to know my friends and my family and me, Hildy, at least a little bit. Kind of be in our shoes, if you know what I mean.

Yours very truly,

Hildy Calpurnia Rose

21 St. Paul's Court

So many people live at 21 St. Paul's Court, it's like a tiny city. My parents, my little brother, Marty, and I live right in the middle of it all, in apartment 4A. Mrs. Tice and her daughter, Alma, keep Winky and a zillion other cats in apartment 3A. My friend Larry teaches his French poodle, Martini, tricks in apartment 3C. My grandparents, Nanny and Harry, play gin and watch the baseball game in 5A. Charlie the super bangs on the pipes across from the elevator in 1D. And that's just for starters.

At night, living in an apartment is a little like being at the movies. The windows are the movie screens, and what happens inside each apartment are the different movies or maybe just different scenes in one big movie called *Apartment Life*. In living color, starring everyone I know.

That's when I love to look out my own window into other people's.

"It's not nice peering in at the neighbors," Dad tells me. "People want their privacy."

So I stop peering, but sometimes I still peek. I watch what Robert Wong is watching on his TV, and I look at Donna Schwartz playing with her Barbie dolls. My friend Christine and I see each other and send a secret message across, which I can't say any more about or it wouldn't be secret.

In the summertime, when everyone has their windows open, I can stick my head out and listen.

"How many times do I have to ask you? Take out the garbage!" Mrs. Fanelli yells.

"You have some mouth on you," Mr. Fanelli yells back. "Try keeping it shut once in a while!"

"Nothing like a hot summer day to get people's tempers boiling," my mom says to herself.

I can hear Mr. Kasbier singing opera and Tandy McNeely singing rock-'n'-roll. At dinnertime, I can hear the silverware clinking against everyone's plates. And I can smell what they're eating. Mrs. Rosetti's tomato sauce uses lots of garlic. She says it keeps away germs and people you don't like.

When I smell Nanny serving dinner, I call her on the intercom. "My crystal ball shows liver and onions in the stars tonight."

"That's right!" she says, surprised. "Come up and join us, Hildy."

"Um...how about dessert?" I answer. Let's just say liver and onions aren't my favorite.

Most of all, I love to go onto the roof of 21 St. Paul's Court, where I can see across to thousands of other buildings, to where millions of other people are living their lives.

"Let's go visit tar beach, Hildy," Mom says on steamy afternoons. And we take our basket of wet clothes to hang them on the line. I feed Mr. Cook's homing pigeons in their little house, then I twirl around in all the space.

"Hey, Mom," I say, squinting out across the rooftop clotheslines. "I see London, I see France, I see Mrs. Haskell's underpants!"

"All I see is one Miss Sillypants," Mom says, looking at me. And we start back downstairs, laughing.

"How about a tall glass of ice tea, Miss Sillypants? Maybe Nanny will join us."

My Best Friend

My best friend, Ruth, and I have known each other since kindergarten. When she sleeps over, we spend most of the time laughing—everything seems so *funny*. Sometimes my father pokes his head in and says, "Cheer up, Ruth!" This makes us laugh even harder until she collapses on the floor, yelling, "Stop, stop, I can't take it anymore!" Then my brother, Marty, jumps on her and gives her noogies.

"Okay, everybody, time to calm down and get ready for bed," Mom says.

She gives Marty cookies and milk to take his mind off Ruth. I hope his cookie crumbs don't bring out the cockroaches.

Ruth sleeps in my bed so we can talk. Peter's party is next Saturday, and our whole class is invited. He can speak Italian, and his parents are artists. I think he's the cat's meow. That means I really, really like him. Ruth thinks Jack is the cat's meow because he makes her laugh. But sometimes they can both be pretty creepy.

"What can you expect? They *are* boys. If I ever get married, it won't be until I'm really old," Ruth says.

"Me, too!" I agree.

In the middle of the night, Ruth gets a nosebleed.

"Uh-oh," I hear her say.

I get her a cool washcloth and hold her head back. It stops soon and we go to sleep again. Then I wake her up when I scream in my sleep. My heart is pounding, and sweat is dripping down my neck.

"Hildy, Hildy, it's okay. You're dreaming," Ruth says, and hugs me.

I hate those stupid nightmares. I don't even know I'm screaming, and I never remember what scared me. Ruth is used to it, though.

"They'll go away one day. You'll see," she says.

I lie down again and think about tomorrow. We'll go to our favorite place, Coney Island. It's like a circus at the beach. People pop out at you there. Tiny people and giant people, thin ones and fat ones, bearded ones who look like ladies and pretty ones who might be men. Ruth and I hold on to each other the whole time.

I'll bring my camera and my journal.

"I wonder if the gypsy lady at Coney Island will be telling fortunes," I whisper to Ruth.

There's no answer. My friend is fast asleep.

Miss Adlonia Frazier

Miss Adlonia Frazier lives in a brownstone with roses all around. Miss Adlonia says, "Roses are just like children. If you're good to them and treat them right, they'll grow and be gorgeous."

Marty and I visit Miss Adlonia a lot. Since she doesn't have any children of her own, she likes us to keep her company. She makes us tall glasses of pink lemonade with ice cubes. "Now sip it slowly, children. We have the whole rest of the day to be hot," she says. "This lemonade is my special recipe. It cools the body and the soul."

Miss Adlonia loves to laugh. When she does, she throws her head way back and closes her eyes. Then she claps her hands a bunch of times. "You've got to laugh, child," she says. "That's how God knows how to find you."

I know Miss Adlonia loves us, because when her friends drop by her garden fence, she says, "I want you to meet some of my children." Then she holds us and gives us kisses.

My mother calls and says, "Miss Adlonia, you're too nice. I'm sure you have more important things you need to do. Tell those kids to come on home." And Miss Adlonia answers, "What's more important than spending a hot afternoon with two of my favorite little roses?"

Aunt Henrietta's Missing Teeth

Sometimes my great-aunt Henrietta acts cuckoo. My grandmother says Aunt Henrietta is afraid of her own shadow. My parents say she isn't really cuckoo, she's just very, very nervous.

When Marty and I visit, we love to look out her living room window. She lives in a tall apartment building, and we can see almost the whole city. But as soon as Aunt Henrietta notices us she starts breathing really fast. "Stay away from that window! You'll fall out!" she yells.

My brother says, "Don't worry, Aunt Henny, it's closed." But Aunt Henrietta's breathing won't slow down unless we sit like statues on the couch, where she can watch us. So we do, and to keep from getting bored, we ask her to tell the story about her missing teeth.

"Well, back when I was a little girl, our family was very poor. My brother Moe, your great-uncle, wanted to be a dentist when he grew up, but it was expensive to go to dental school. So I had an idea. I made a deal with the tooth fairy. When she came for my teeth, she could take as many as she wanted — *if* she left a lot of money under Moe's pillow for dental school. Well, she took all my choppers, and that's how Moe became a dentist."

Aunt Henrietta winks at the end of the story and lights one of her Lucky Strikes. I wonder how she *really* lost her teeth.

The Baby-sitters

"Now *come on,* Hildy," my dad says when Mrs. Shoenberg is our baby-sitter. "She's not so bad."

"She might be fun to describe in your journal," Mom says, putting on her coat. "Be good now, my dumplings. Smooch smooch." And they leave.

Marty and I look at each other and roll our eyes. Mom's right about one thing, though. I do like writing about baby-sitters. It's something to do instead of going crazy when I'm stuck with them. And usually I can find out important character traits—like, are they mean, friendly, weird?

For example, all Mrs. Shoenberg ever wants to do is read her old newspapers and drink tonic water all night long. She has gray hair with yellow tinges and wears a pencil behind her ear to do crossword puzzles.

Connie used to baby-sit. She was skinny, and one front tooth was solid gold. Once she fell asleep on my parents' bed, watching the fights on TV. Then we stared at her, and I don't even think it was rude, since she didn't know we were staring. Dad says it's still rude even if the person's asleep, because they can't protect themselves from your eyes. Turns out she drank too much alcohol.

Connie never came back after that, but Mrs. Goddard did. She wore gobs of powder on her face and looked like a plump ghost. She taught us card games like Pisha Peysha, but she smoked a ton of cigarettes, and I got sick and threw up.

Martine from Argentina is our favorite baby-sitter. She teaches us songs in Spanish and makes coffee the Argentinian way. She smells good, too, and loves to play games.

If Martine can't baby-sit, her roommate Monique from France usually can. My brother says, "Oh, Monique, ooh la la." He thinks she's beautiful.

Pretty soon I'll be too old for baby-sitters. Will I miss them? Um…NO!

The Schlag Test

My family has been going to Peter Luger's Steak House in Williamsburg, Brooklyn, for four generations. Most of the waiters are German, including Carl, the maître d'. He's my father's close friend.

"Ach, Herr Gott im himmel, so nice to see you. Your table is ready down in the basement," Carl jokes.

"Who made the schlag tonight?" my father asks. "Is it real, or is it Cool Whip?" he teases.

"Schlag" is the German word for thick whipped cream, which is delicious on top of warm homemade apple pie.

Wolf, our waiter, laughs all the way through our dinner. He knows my father is going to do the schlag test at dessert.

Finally, we're finished. Marty's and my eyes are on the swinging kitchen doors. We can see Rudi, the expert schlag maker, peering out the little window, and we make our schlag faces. Rudi winks at me. Plates of apple pie come out on Wolf's arms—and a beautiful big bowl of schlag! He puts it down in front of my father.

"Alan, you're not...are you?" pleads Mom. But before she can finish her sentence, Dad takes the bowl of schlag and turns it completely upside down in the air! The restaurant is suddenly quiet. Not a drop falls. My father turns the bowl right side up again, gives the thumbs-up sign, and grins. Everybody laughs with relief, and claps.

"I guess Rudi made the schlag tonight," my father says.

I look back at the little window in the kitchen door. Rudi is laughing too. The schlag test is over.

My Friend Hank

Hank DiPaolo is a grownup, and he is my friend. He lives in my building on the first floor. "Hi there, cutie," he says when he sees me. "How's life treating you? Read any good books? Are you married yet?"

"No, silly." I laugh.

"You're the only one for me," he says. "Well, hop on, what are you waiting for?"

I run and jump on his lap. Then the two of us go for a ride in his wheelchair.

A few nights ago I dreamed Hank and I were dancing. We were whirling in circles, and he picked me way up high like a ballerina. My parents were clapping and laughing as we danced around and around.

When Hank and his wife, Lena, invited me over for dinner last night, I told them my dream. Hank held my hand and didn't say anything for a long time.

"Hildy, sweetheart, I did used to dance like that. I taught ballroom dancing before I had my accident."

"I didn't know that," I said.

"That's how Lena and I met. We were both instructors at the same school. You should've seen us. We were smooth."

Lena smiled. "Hank was quite a hoofer."

"What do you mean *was*?" Hank said. "These wheels can do some pretty fancy moves, you know. Here, Hildy, hop on."

Lena put "Rainy Nights in Spain" on the stereo, and Hank put his cheek to mine. We stretched our arms out, holding hands. We were doing the tango. "Excuse me, may I cut in?" Lena said.

She climbed on, too, and the three of us made a sandwich with me in the middle. When the music stopped, Hank and Lena kissed on the lips. I hopped off and got the dessert I brought—tortoni ice cream and cannolis. I gave Hank and Lena a cannoli. Hank bit one end and Lena bit the other. When they got to the middle, they kissed again. I turned the record over and climbed on Hank's wheelchair back into our sandwich. This time we danced the samba. "Bravo, bravo!" Hank yelled. "What a life!"

Dear Reader,

It's almost midnight now. I just finished writing the last pages in my journal. Mom saw the light coming from under my covers when she walked by my room.

"Hildy, are you still awake?"

"I'm finished now, Mom," I whisper, turning off the flashlight and putting the cap on my fountain pen.

"Hildy Calpurnia Rose," she says in her pretend angry voice, "you are going to go blind writing under your covers like that."

"Yes, Mom," I agree.

She tucks me in again and kisses me on both cheeks. She smells good.

"Good night, my girl. See you in the morning." She tiptoes over to Marty's bed and kisses him twice too, even though he's asleep.

Tomorrow after school I'll go to Irv's Stationery Store for a new journal. I have a lot more stories to write down. Oh, and I'd better get some flashlight batteries, too.

Good night for now,

Hildy Calpurnia Rose